AMERICAN WAR BIOGRAPHIES

John Paul Jones

Karen Price Hossell

Heinemann Library
Chicago, Illinois

©2004 Heinemann Library
a division of Reed Elsevier Inc.
Chicago, Illinois

Customer Service 888-454-2279
Visit our website at www.heinemannlibrary.com

Designed by Heinemann Library
Page layout by Lisa Buckley
Maps by John Fleck
Photo research by Janet Lankford Moran
Printed and bound in China by South China Printing
   Company Limited

08 07 06 05 04
10 9 8 7 6 5 4 3 2 1

Library of Congress Cataloging-in-Publication Data
Price Hossell, Karen, 1957-
   John Paul Jones / Karen Price Hossell.
       p. cm. -- (American war biographies)
   Summary: Profiles Scottish-American sailor John Paul Jones, discussing his accomplishments in the Continental Navy during the Revolutionary War and his later years in Paris and as a member of the Russian Navy.
   Includes bibliographical references (p.) and index.
   ISBN 1-4034-5079-X (lib. bdg.) -- ISBN 1-4034-5086-2 (pbk.)
   1. Jones, John Paul, 1747-1792--Juvenile literature. 2. Admirals--United States--Biography--Juvenile literature. 3. United States. Navy--Biography--Juvenile literature. 4. United States--History--Revolution, 1775-1783--Naval operations--Juvenile literature. [1. Jones, John Paul, 1747-1792. 2. Admirals. 3. United States.--Navy--Biography. 4. United States--History--Revolution, 1775-1783.] I. Title. II. Series.
   E207.J7P75 2004
   973.3'5'092--dc22
                              2003021786

Acknowledgments
The author and publisher are grateful to the following for permission to reproduce copyright material:
pp. 5, 25, 27, 29 National Archives and Records Administration; p. 7 Historical Picture Archive/Corbis; p. 9 Bill Lealman/Filey, UK; p. 10 Hulton Archive/Getty Images; pp. 13, 19, 20, 34, 42 Library of Congress; p. 15 Private Collection/Archives Charment/Bridgeman Art Library; p. 16 Courtesy of the U.S. Navy Art Collection, Washington, D.C. Donation of the Memphis Council, U.S. Navy League, 1976/U.S. Naval Historical Center Photograph; pp. 24, 31, 41 North Wind Picture Archives; p. 33 The Granger Collection, New York; p. 36 Bettmann/Corbis; p. 37 Archivo Iconografico, S. A./Corbis; p. 39 Alexander Burkatowski/Corbis; p. 43 Paul A. Souders/Corbis

Cover photograph by Library of Congress

Special thanks to Gary Barr for his help in the preparation of this book.

Every effort has been made to contact copyright holders of any material reproduced in this book. Any omissions will be rectified in subsequent printings if notice is given to the publisher.

Some words are shown in bold, **like this.** You can find out what they mean by looking in the glossary.

Contents

1 The Revolutionary War

The Revolutionary War was fought between American **colonists** and the British. It began on April 19, 1775, with a battle at Lexington, Massachusetts, and officially ended in 1783.

The American **colonies** were settled by Great Britain, and colonists were required to follow laws passed by Britain's top lawmaking body, called **Parliament.** In the early years of settlement, few colonists questioned this. But in the mid-1700s, Parliament began passing laws that angered many Americans. Parliament also began forcing colonists to pay taxes on many items. Because Great Britain did not allow Americans to be a part of Parliament, the colonists had no way to protest these laws and taxes except to write or speak out against them.

Patriots and Loyalists

In the years leading up to the Revolutionary War, American colonists were becoming divided into two groups. One group, called **Loyalists,** believed that the colonies should remain a part of Great Britain. The other group was the **Patriots.** Many Patriots wanted to break all ties with Great Britain and form a nation that governed itself. Others felt at first that the colonies could remain tied to Great Britain, but that they should have more freedom.

The Boston Tea Party

Since they had little say in the way they were governed and no vote in Parliament, American colonists became frustrated with their failure to be heard by Great Britain. So on December 16, 1773, American Patriots found a new way to get Britain's attention by staging the Boston Tea Party in Boston, Massachusetts. To protest the tea tax, they boarded ships carrying tea and threw the tea into Boston Harbor. Parliament punished the Patriots for their actions by ordering British troops to move into

In some of the first fighting of the Revolutionary War, American colonists chased British soldiers across Concord's North Bridge on April 19, 1775.

Boston to make sure that nothing like this happened again. Then Parliament closed Boston Harbor, which meant that the British controlled which ships sailed in and out. By April of 1775, tensions had risen even more. Patriots who had once thought that the colonies could be content under British rule were changing their minds and agreeing with those who wanted complete independence from Great Britain.

Lexington and Concord

On April 19, 1775, the first battles of the Revolutionary War occurred when about 70 **militiamen** from Massachusetts faced British soldiers who were advancing on Lexington Green. The British troops were on their way to the city of Concord, following orders from British General Gage to destroy the weapons warehouse there. Gage had ordered about 700 British troops to Concord. Those marching into Lexington were advance troops, sent ahead to find out what kind of situation the rest of the soldiers would face.

It is not known which side fired first, but a shot rang out. The British fired at the militiamen and then charged them with **bayonets.** When the fighting was over, eight Americans were dead and ten were wounded. The British continued on to Concord. After destroying the weapons warehouse, they met up with another group of Americans at Concord's North Bridge. Three British soldiers were killed in fighting there. The fighting at Lexington and Concord marked the start of the Revolutionary War.

The Continental army

The war was fought on land by the Continental army. It was made up of volunteers, many of them from local **militia** groups. Led by General George Washington, the army was started by the **Continental Congress,** which was the lawmaking body of the American colonies.

In 1775 the Continental army had a long and difficult task. The British had a large and powerful army and sent thousands of soldiers to the colonies to force Americans to stop fighting for independence. The Continental army, on the other hand, was made up of militias and volunteers from the thirteen colonies. While the British had an experienced, well-trained army, the Continentals were inexperienced and had little money to buy weapons and supplies.

The Continental navy

The armies fought their battles on land, but there was also activity on the sea. With about 270 ships, the British navy was one of the largest and most powerful forces in the world. It used its ships to transport soldiers and supplies for its army from England to the colonies and to control areas such as Boston Harbor and other American rivers, lakes, and harbors.

At the beginning of the war, the Americans had only a small navy made up of a few ships. It was nearly useless against the British fleet. Many members of the Continental Congress saw little need for a Continental navy. Congress could barely scrape together enough money for the Continental army. Finding the money, supplies, and men needed to form a navy of any size seemed like an impossible task.

In October 1775, however, Congress voted to turn two ships into naval **cruisers** and to begin building a larger naval force. Congress appointed a seven-person Marine Committee—also known as the Naval Committee—

The British first-rate ship of the line could carry over 100 guns and 800 crew. It was considered the greatest warship of its day.

to decide how the navy could best be organized. Among the committee members were future United States President John Adams from Massachusetts, Silas Deane from Connecticut, and Joseph Hewes from North Carolina. On November 25, 1775, the Committee ordered the small navy to begin capturing British ships. Committee members then began to appoint officers. One of the first officers selected by the committee was John Paul Jones. He went on to become a great naval hero; someone who was praised by Americans and hated by the British.

2 Early Life

There was little in John Paul's childhood (he took the name "Jones" later) that gave a clue as to how famous he would be later in life. He was born on July 6, 1747, in Kirkcudbrightshire, Scotland. John's father was a gardener at Arbigland, the large estate of a wealthy man named William Craik. John, his parents, his brother, and his three sisters lived in a two-room cottage on the banks of the Firth of Solway, which is a bay in the southern part of Scotland. John spent his early years running around the estate and playing with his brothers and sisters and the children of Craik's other employees. One story about Jones says that as a young boy he sometimes told his friends to get into rowboats and paddle about in the sea. John Paul would then stand on a rock on the shore and shout orders to his friends as they played on the water.

In those days, most young men whose fathers were not wealthy went to school only until they were twelve or thirteen. They usually learned only basic subjects, such as reading, writing, and mathematics. Then they left school to learn a skill by becoming **apprentices.** They signed on to work with men already established in a trade or a business, usually for about seven years. When they were finished, apprentices knew everything they needed about their trade, and most continued on in that kind of work for the rest of their lives.

Apprenticeship

Some young men, such as John Paul, were drawn to the sea, and they signed on to work on ships. When he was thirteen John found work as an apprentice aboard the ship

Visitors to Arbigland, Scotland, can visit the John Paul Jones Cottage Museum and see how the young John Paul and his family lived in the 1700s.

Friendship, which sailed out of Whitehaven, England. He had hoped to join England's Royal Navy right away, but young boys who wanted to join the navy had to know someone who could help them get in, and Jones knew no one.

Jones had many duties on board the ship. Sometimes he would mop the decks of the ship, or coil the large ropes that were used on board. Perhaps his most dangerous duty was to climb the *Friendship's* tall masts and gather the sails. Many sailors were killed doing this—the masts were often unsteady as the ship rocked back and forth with the waves, and sailors would lose their balance and fall to the deck or into the ocean.

John loved ships and everything about them. He was a quick learner and serious about his chosen profession. Throughout his life he was known as one of the neatest, most precise sailors in the navy.

By the time John was seventeen, he had crossed the Atlantic Ocean eight times. But the same year he turned seventeen, the owners of the *Friendship* needed money, so they sold the ship. Now John had to find work on another ship. He found a job as **third mate** on the *King George*. In later life, John rarely spoke about his years on the *King George* and the next ship he worked on, *Two Friends*. In fact, he preferred to forget about his experience on those ships altogether, because the *King George* and *Two Friends* were slave ships.

Slave ships

Because he rarely, if ever, wrote or spoke about his time on slave ships, we know little of what John Paul experienced. But life on board a slave ship was always horrifying. It was most miserable, of course, for those who were kidnapped from their homes in Africa and forced to board the ships. The misery of the slaves filled the entire ship and affected the crew, as well. If they were not that way already, after living in these conditions for so long, many crew members became extremely cruel and often mistreated the slaves.

To make sure they made as much money as possible from each ship, slave ship owners packed as many people on the ships as they could. The hands and feet of the slaves were not only chained together, but the slaves were chained to one another, sometimes in pairs and sometimes in larger

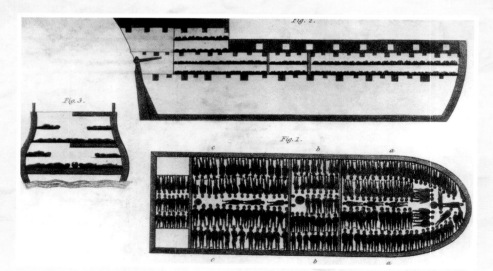

This diagram of an 18th-century slave ship shows how crowded it was for the African slaves in the cargo hold. Conditions were so horrible that at least 25 percent of the slaves, on average, would die before a ship reached its destination.

Olaudah Equiano's story

A man named Olaudah Equiano was captured in his homeland of Benin, Africa, and became a slave in the 1700s. In 1789 he wrote *The Life of Olaudah Equiano the African.* Below is his description of his voyage to America from Africa.

I was soon put down under the decks, and there I received such a greeting in my nostrils as I had never experienced in my life; so that, with the loathsomeness [awfulness] of the stench, and crying together, I became so sick and low that I was not able to eat, nor had I the least desire to taste anything. . . . The white people looked and acted, as I thought, in so savage a manner; for I had never seen among my people such instances of brutal cruelty. The closeness of the place, and the heat of the climate, added to the number in the ship, which was so crowded that each had scarcely room to turn himself, almost suffocated us. The air soon became unfit for respiration [breathing], from a variety of loathsome smells, and brought on a sickness among the slaves, of which many died. . . . The shrieks of the women, and the groans of the dying, rendered the whole a scene of horror almost inconceivable [impossible to believe].

groups. The slaves were forced below deck and made to lie down. They were kept in that position during almost the entire voyage, which usually lasted about three to four weeks. Sometimes slaves had to lie on top of one another. There was little chance for fresh air to get into the holds, and there were no bathrooms, only tubs that many slaves could not reach. The slave quarters on board ship were rarely cleaned during a voyage. Sometimes, if the weather was good, slaves were allowed to go up to the top deck, where they were fed. Because the conditions were so bad—and because they were terrified of what lay ahead—many slaves tried to kill themselves by jumping into the sea or refusing to eat.

While the *Two Friends* was docked in Jamaica in 1767, John Paul walked away from the ship, vowing never to get back on board. He went back to Scotland on a ship called *John.* During the voyage, both the captain and the ship's first mate died. No one else on board knew how to navigate well enough to get the ship back to Scotland—that is, no one but John Paul. He took over and brought the *John* safely back home. In Scotland, the ship's owners were so pleased with his accomplishment that they gave him command of the ship. He was only 21 years old.

3 Trouble at Sea

Under the command of John Paul, the small crew of *John* kept what is called a "tight ship." Captain Paul was particular about everything and insisted that the ship be kept clean and that all the equipment be in good shape. He made his crew work hard, and he was very demanding.

Mungo Maxwell

Mungo Maxwell, one of the men on the *John*'s crew, thought Captain Paul was often too demanding. One day Maxwell refused to follow orders. He talked back to John Paul, so Paul had him flogged. When sailors were flogged, they were beaten with nine strands of thick rope that had a

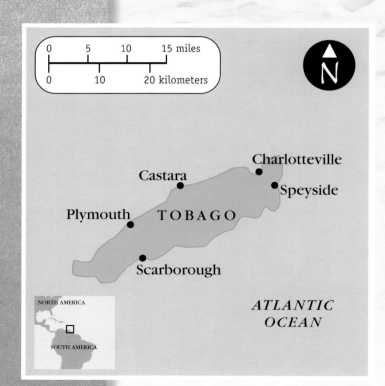

The island of Tobago is now part of the country of Trinidad and Tobago. During the 17th, 18th, and 19th centuries, thousands of slaves were brought from Africa to work on the island's plantations.

series of knots tied into them. The number of times they were flogged depended on how serious their offense was.

Flogging was a common punishment on board any **merchant** ship, so Paul's actions were not unusual. But when the ship reached **Tobago,** Maxwell decided to complain to the officials there. A judge listened to both Maxwell's and Paul's story of the incident and decided that Paul was not wrong to have Maxwell flogged. The angry Maxwell then quit the crew and sailed back to Scotland on another ship. Captain Paul returned to Scotland on the *John*.

Masons

John Paul Jones became a Mason, or Freemason, in 1770. No one is exactly sure when the Masons began—many believe the group started with the **guilds** of **stonemasons.** In 1717, Masons in England formally organized. Many early American leaders were Masons, including George Washington. Masons help one another out whenever they can, and the connections Jones made after he became a member of this group helped him when he was in Virginia and throughout his life.

When he arrived in Scotland, however, Paul was shocked when he was immediately arrested for murder. Maxwell had died on the voyage to Scotland, and John Paul was accused of beating him so harshly that Maxwell died of his wounds. The Maxwell family, which was a powerful and wealthy Scottish family, insisted that John Paul be punished. Later, though, the captain of the ship on which Maxwell died said that he had died of a fever, not of his beating, so John Paul was allowed to go free.

The Ringleader

Another incident occurred soon after that one, when John Paul was commanding the *Betsy*. The *John* had been sold, and John Paul was put in charge of the *Betsy* in 1772. While on a voyage, he argued with a crew member. The man, whom John Paul called only "the Ringleader" when he wrote about it later, was angry that he and the other crewmen had not been paid. Paul said the Ringleader was going to persuade the crew to take over the ship. John Paul went into his quarters to get a stick, or so he said. But he claimed that his sword just happened to be on the table, so he picked that up instead. The Ringleader, holding a heavy wooden stick, came toward John Paul. They fought until Captain Paul was cornered. He raised his sword, and he said that the Ringleader ran into it and died from his wound.

Because he knew he would have to answer for the Ringleader's death, John Paul sailed to nearby **Tobago** and turned himself in to the authorities there. He thought he would be tried by an admiralty court, which is a court that deals with cases that relate to the sea. But the admiralty court was not in session. Instead Paul would have to go before the local court. And as it turned out, the Ringleader was from Tobago, so the men that would have been on the **jury** would be his countrymen—some might have even known him. John Paul already knew that the locals were upset about the Ringleader's death. He decided he had no chance for a fair trial, and he feared he would be convicted and hanged. So he ran away. He ended up in Virginia, and once there he decided to add "Jones" to his name to protect his identity.

This painting of John Paul Jones was done at the height of his fame and naval career. He is wearing a medal given to him by King Louis XVI of France.

4 Jones and the Continental Navy

John Paul Jones had always hoped to settle someday in Virginia. He saw himself living on a large **plantation** in a comfortable home. While in Virginia, John Paul Jones read books, hoping to educate himself so that he would fit into society. He also paid close attention to the war, which had just begun. He knew that the **Continental Congress** was organizing an army under the leadership of George Washington. Congress also talked about building up its tiny navy, but because it had so little money it had not made much progress. In the late summer or early fall of 1775, Jones traveled to Philadelphia to meet with Congress. He told them that he was an experienced sailor and that he would like to serve in the Continental navy.

Congress was not yet ready to hire naval officers, but John's name was put on a list of prospects. In the meantime, Congress decided that it needed at least thirteen new ships, so it arranged to have them built. While those ships were being built, Congress looked around for other ships it could use, then began naming men to command them. On December 7, 1775, Jones

1775

Fall
Jones goes to Philadelphia to ask to be in Continental navy

December
He is made first lieutenant on the *Alfred*

1776

May
Made captain of the sloop *Providence*

November
Given command of *Alfred* again

The Grand Union flag

On December 3, 1775, First Lieutenant John Paul Jones raised the Grand Union flag on the *Alfred*. This was the first time a flag representing the American colonies was raised on a Continental warship. This early American flag design—one of several—combined American patriotism with loyalty to Great Britain. In the upper left corner was a Union Jack, representing Great Britain and loyalty to the king. But the flag's thirteen stripes stood for the thirteen colonies united against British **tyranny**.

got his wish to be in the navy when he was made first lieutenant aboard the *Alfred.* The *Alfred* was 100 feet (30 meters) long and 35 feet (10 meters) wide. It was painted black with a yellow stripe.

Jones saw little excitement in his first months as a naval officer. But in May of 1776, he was made the captain of a sloop called *Providence,* which was to escort merchant ships. Now he commanded his own ship for the Continental navy.

Seizing British ships

The naval committee instructed Jones to begin cruising against British ships. This meant that he was to look for and capture British supply ships. Because he would be stopping the flow of supplies to the British army in the colonies, he would be helping America win the war. To motivate naval officers to capture ships, Congress gave captains bonus money, some of which was to go to the crew, for every ship they seized. And there were plenty of British ships on the Atlantic for Jones and other officers to go after. In July and August of 1776, for example, about 130 British ships sailed into New York Harbor. They went to New York because at the time the city was controlled by the British.

See the *Providence*

Visitors to Providence, Rhode Island, can see a replica of the sloop *Providence* docked there. The original *Providence* was 70 feet (21 meters) long and was manned by a crew of 73.

Jones loved excitement, and he loved sailing. He and his crew eagerly set out to prowl the Atlantic for British ships. They sailed the *Providence* to the waters near Bermuda, for example, where they captured three British ships and led one on a thrilling ten-hour chase. By October 7, the *Providence* had captured sixteen British supply ships, although it brought back only six of them as prizes. The others were burned, sunk, or recaptured by the British.

Mission to Nova Scotia

On November 1, 1776, the head of the navy, **Commodore** Hopkins, made Jones captain of the *Alfred*. He told Jones to go to Nova Scotia, an island off the northern coast of Maine, and rescue Americans who were being held as prisoners there. Most of the Americans were soldiers who were captured by the British during the war. Because Nova Scotia was British territory, they were being kept there.

For this mission Jones led a small fleet of ships. Besides the *Alfred*, the ship he now captained, he was in charge of the *Providence* and the *Hampden*. As commander of the fleet he had the title of commodore.

On his voyage to Nova Scotia, Jones came across a **privateer** and forced some of the men on board to join his crew. The men had **deserted** from the navy to be privateers, so Jones felt he had the right to make them return to the navy, and he needed them to help man his ships.

Privateers

John Paul Jones captured British ships for the American navy, but about 2,000 ships that sailed during the Revolution were privateers. The American government gave privateers permission to seize enemy ships and keep what they found. They benefited the war effort by taking supplies meant for the British army and the ships that transported them.

At first the mission went well. Jones and his crew were able to seize the British ship *Mellish*. Aboard the ship were 10,000 winter uniforms to be used by the British army. The warm uniforms went to the Continental army instead, which desperately needed them. But not long after this victory, the ships ran into bad weather, with huge waves and high winds. The crew members of the *Providence* decided that they did not want to stay in the dangerous waters around Nova Scotia.

Then Jones discovered that the prisoners he had come to rescue had all joined the British army. This was not all that unusual during the Revolution. Prison conditions were harsh, and the prisoners in Nova Scotia were forced to work in coal pits. Joining the enemy meant that they would at least have a fairly comfortable place to sleep. Because they had joined the British, however, Jones no longer had a mission, so he returned home. First, however, he and his men seized British ships bringing coal from Nova Scotia to New York. The **seizure** meant that the British would have trouble keeping warm that winter.

When he arrived in Portsmouth, Jones was charged with **piracy** for boarding the privateer and forcing men on board to join his crew. The command of the *Alfred* was taken away from him, and he was given back his old ship, the *Providence*.

5   Jones Proposes a Plan

John Paul Jones loved glory more than anything. He wanted people to notice him and to reward him for his work on the seas. But the **Continental Congress** did not often reward people just for their work alone. Instead, they gave honors to relatives, to friends, to friends of friends, and to people to whom they owed favors. That is why Jones, who already had a reputation as a great sailor, was passed over for **promotion** in 1776. Men who had done less for the **Patriot** cause and who had less experience at sea were given command of better ships. Jones, on the other hand, was put in charge of slow, old ships.

The plan

But while this hurt and angered Jones, it did not stop his belief in American independence and in his own ability to help achieve it. In fact, Jones came up with a way the navy could further help win the war, and on March 7, 1777, he went to Congress with his plan. He thought it would be a

The United States

The American colonies officially became the United States on July 4, 1776, when the Declaration of Independence was announced to the world. In the Declaration is a sentence that reads: "these United Colonies are, and of Right ought to be Free and Independent States." With the Declaration of Independence, the American people were showing that the colonies—now states—were determined to band together to work as one nation for freedom from Great Britain.

Phillis Wheatley

While Congress was considering Jones's plan for invading the British coast, he went to Boston, where he mingled with people of society at parties and elegant dinners. One woman Jones got to know while he was in Boston was Phillis Wheatley. Perhaps they met because they were both poets—Jones enjoyed writing poetry, although is work is not considered as good as Wheatley's. Wheatley was an African American who was named after the slave ship in which she sailed to America. She was born in Africa in about 1753. When she was seven, she was kidnapped from her family in Africa and sent to Boston, where a wealthy family named Wheatley bought her. They took her in as one of their own children and taught her not only reading and writing, but also Greek and Latin. Phillis was a quick learner who liked poetry. Her poems became known in the 1760s, and as a young lady she was accepted into Boston society, attending parties and balls. Most likely she met John Paul Jones at one of these events. Her poems became known in Europe, and she traveled to England in the early 1770s. In 1773, a book of her poetry was published in England. Phillis was also given her freedom in 1773, and in 1778 she was married. She died in 1784.

good idea to send a fleet of ships, which he would command, to sail along the coast of Great Britain. The fleet could attack areas that were not defended. He believed that this would result in two things. First, the British navy would be forced to sail ships away from the United States back to Great Britain to protect the people who lived along the coast. Second, the attacks would strike fear into the British people. Except for the soldiers sent to the United States and the **Loyalists** who lived there, the people of Great Britain had not been directly involved in the Revolutionary War. Jones wanted to bring some of the war to them, and he hoped that doing this would force the British people to plead with their government to stop fighting for the colonies. If enough people pressured the government to do this, the war could soon end, and the United States would be free. Finally, Jones wanted to capture as many British prisoners as he could and then work out a prisoner exchange to free American prisoners of war.

The *Ranger,* commanded by John Paul Jones, is receiving a nine-gun salute from the French ship, *La Motte Picquet,* off of Quiberon Bay on February 12, 1778.

Not long after his visit to Congress, Jones was instructed to go to France. Congress had decided that his plan to attack towns along the British coast was a good one. In France, Jones was to meet with the American **commissioners** Benjamin Franklin, Silas Deane, and Arthur Lee. They would give him a ship that he could use to carry out his plan.

Prisoner of war exchanges

Prisoner of war exchanges were not uncommon during the Revolutionary War. Leaders from each side would **negotiate** terms for the release of prisoners from their country. The terms would be in writing and could be somewhat complicated. They could sometimes resemble a game—for example, the terms might say that ten "common" prisoners could be exchanged for one colonel, or forty prisoners for a colonel and a general.

The *Ranger*

The ship Jones was given to sail to France was the *Ranger*. Once he had his ship, Jones began to recruit sailors to help him carry out his warfare. The *Ranger* and its crew left Portsmouth, New Hampshire, on November 1, 1777. As the ship approached France, Jones saluted a French ship by hoisting the Stars and Stripes, representing the United States of America. The salute was

Edward Bancroft

John Paul Jones met Edward Bancroft in Paris, where Bancroft was Benjamin Franklin's friend. Jones and Bancroft became friends and wrote many letters to each other. What Jones did not know was that Bancroft was a double agent, acting as a spy for both the Americans and the British. Thinking he was writing to a friend, Jones gave Bancroft information about his plans, and Bancroft passed some of them along to the British. Bancroft was also a scientist. His career as a spy was not revealed until 1891, when historian and writer Paul L. Ford researched him and wrote about his discoveries.

returned by French Admiral La Motte-Picquet, making that the first time an American ship was recognized by a foreign country.

In France, Jones discovered that the ship he had hoped to get had been sold instead to the Dutch, so he decided to continue using the *Ranger*. He prepared the ship for his raids by having new, lighter masts made so that it would not **capsize**—the original masts were too big. Jones also disguised the ship by hanging giant strips of red cloth over its sides to hide the guns. On April 8, 1778, the *Ranger* set out for Great Britain.

Jones planned to stop at British port towns and terrorize them by threatening to burn them. He also planned to kidnap important men in the towns and hold them for **ransom** until Americans who were being held in British prisons were set free. But not everyone in the crew of the *Ranger* went along with this plan, and they threatened **mutiny.** One reason the sailors were angry was that in France, they had to wait on board the ship while Jones took care of business and other matters in Paris. Among the "other matters" were parties and love affairs. The sailors on the *Ranger* disliked having to remain on the ship while Jones enjoyed himself. To make matters worse, one of the sailors had **smallpox,** a dangerous disease feared by everyone in the 1700s. When people got smallpox, blister-like sores appeared all over their bodies, and sometimes they died. The disease spread quickly, especially in the close quarters of a ship. Because of the unrest on the ship, Jones became so concerned that his men would toss him overboard or even kill him outright that he barely slept at all for several weeks.

6 Terrorizing the British

As Jones and his crew sailed in the Irish Sea between Scotland and Ireland, they found several small ships, which they captured as prizes. But while Jones was pleased to have captured these ships, he was more concerned with his next big plan. He intended to go to the fishing village of Whitehaven on the northwest coast of England. In the harbor there were many **merchantmen,** and Jones planned to attack in the dead of night, burn all the ships, and escape before dawn. Because there were two fortresses overlooking the harbor, Jones planned to have some of his men climb up to the forts and spike the cannons there. When they spiked cannons, they drove large nails into the ignition vents so that the cannons would not work.

One reason Jones chose Whitehaven as a target was that he knew the layout of the waters around the town. The ship he **apprenticed** on as a boy had sailed from there. He knew he could find the way through the waters in the dark.

When Jones announced his intentions to his crew, they were not happy. Because they received a small amount of money every time a ship was seized, they wanted to concentrate on taking ships, not burning them. Jones stood before them and made a long speech, hoping to persuade them to go along with his plan. Finally, he was able to get 30 men to volunteer.

The raid

The plan did not work as well as Jones hoped it would. The raiders had trouble sailing from the *Ranger* to Whitehaven, so they did not reach their target until almost dawn. They first scaled the walls of the forts by climbing on one another's shoulder's. The guards were so surprised to see them that they instantly gave in to Jones and his men, who immediately began to spike the cannons. Jones was so busy that he barely noticed that as he and others were spiking the cannons, many of his men disappeared. Soon, though, he found out where they had gone. As he tried to burn the ships with the few men who had stayed with him, a group of drunken sailors—his own missing men— suddenly appeared, laughing and shouting. They had found a **tavern** and had had quite a bit of **ale** to drink.

The drunken men were of little help to Jones as he tried to burn the ships. In fact, only one ship was burned, and that was set ablaze by Jones himself. It helped that the ship was a collier—a coal-carrying ship. Because coal is fuel, once the ship caught fire, it blazed brightly. But Jones and his men could burn no more ships because townspeople were starting to come out of their homes. He discovered later that one of the men who had

This map shows the location of Whitehaven on the west coast of England. At the time of the raid, it was Great Britain's third busiest port.

Jones's uniforms

John Paul Jones probably had little trouble convincing others that he was a British naval officer. He liked to dress in the same kind of uniform British naval officers wore. Even though Congress had decided that American naval captains should wear a blue jacket, blue pants, and a red waistcoat (vest), when going into battle Jones would wear a blue coat, white pants, and white waistcoat.

volunteered to attack Whitehaven really did not care about burning the ships. He had joined Captain Jones's crew only because he wanted to get from America to Ireland. In Whitehaven, he ran down the streets of the village, knocking on doors to wake residents and warn them about the attackers. As people began to gather on the shore overlooking the harbor, Jones and his men decided to escape. They ran to the boats they had used to sail from *Ranger,* hopped aboard, and rowed back to the ship.

Another plan

The attack did not go nearly as well as Jones had hoped. He had planned to burn all of the ships, but managed to set only one on fire. Jones quickly came up with a new plan. He would go to St. Mary's Isle in Scotland's Firth of Solway and kidnap the Earl of Selkirk. The Earl lived on a large estate, and Jones hoped that kidnapping someone well-known would bring him the praise he wanted.

Jones, along with twelve other men from his crew, rowed to St. Mary's Isle and walked to the estate. Along the way they met up with the estate's gardener, who asked them what they wanted. Jones told the gardener that he was from the British navy and was there to **recruit** men for the navy.

The gardener quickly ran off to warn the other men who worked on the estate, and they all hid. They did not want to be forced to join the navy and live the hard life of a sailor. Now Jones and his men could walk right up to the Earl's large home without worrying about whether the male employees of the estate would try to stop them.

There was one problem, however. The gardener had mentioned that the Earl was away on vacation. His wife, Lady Selkirk, was home, but she was

France's role in the war

In 1776, Benjamin Franklin was sent to Paris to persuade the French to assist the United States in its war with Great Britain. On May 4, 1778, Congress made its first **alliance** with a foreign nation when it agreed to two treaties with France. In one, France recognized American independence and promised to send French soldiers to help in the fight. The other allowed Americans to trade freely with France and all countries it held in its possession. The involvement of the French navy in 1780 helped General George Washington trap British troops between land and sea in Yorktown, Virginia, and resulted in the British surrender to the Continental army.

Benjamin Franklin was 70 years old when he sailed to France. While he was there, Franklin managed to charm the French and became so popular that crowds would follow him in the streets.

not nearly as important as her husband and, in Jones's mind, not worth kidnapping. So he told his men that they might as well go back to the *Ranger*.

The sailors, however, wanted excitement. They had gotten this far, they told Jones, so how could they simply walk away from the prizes that would be in the unprotected house?

Jones did not want his men to go near the house, but he knew that if he told them to go back to the ship they would become violent, and perhaps even burn the house and hurt those who lived there. The sailors were determined to find treasure, so Jones thought for a minute, then decided on a **compromise.** Two officers from the ship would force their way into the Earl's home and demand that they be given his best silver. But they must not, he warned, touch anyone inside the home or treat anyone roughly. Jones did not go to the house. Instead, he waited on the path leading down to the shore.

The others went along with his plan. They figured that the silver would be worth a great deal of money, and that they could sell it and divide up the profits. So the men entered the home and told Lady Selkirk to give them her silver. Lady Selkirk and her servants quickly ran from room to room, gathering up the silver and putting it into a large sack they had found. Then the two officers politely said goodbye and walked away.

The *Drake*

The news of Jones and his crimes quickly spread throughout England. People began to panic as the stories of what Jones and his gang had done became wilder with each telling. The British navy sent out two warships to look for the *Ranger,* but Jones did not want to escape until he had captured another prize. He knew that the British warship *Drake* was anchored in the harbor at Carrickfergus, across the Irish Sea in Ireland. He quietly sailed close to it. The *Drake* sent out a small boat to find out what the *Ranger* wanted—she appeared to be a British ship because Jones was now flying a British flag. When the officer on the boat first saw Jones, he noticed that Jones was wearing a British officer's uniform, so he climbed aboard the *Ranger*. Jones told the officer and the six men who were with him that they were now American prisoners of war.

Then Jones drew the *Ranger* up along the *Drake* and ordered his ship's guns fired. The ships fought for an hour, until the captain of the badly damaged *Drake* surrendered. Jones then took possession of the *Drake,* one of his greatest prizes so far.

The attacks on the British had their desired effect. The people who lived along the coast of Great Britain feared daily that Jones and his vicious mob of crazed pirates would attack their villages. His legend grew into one of a wild-eyed pirate with a long black beard; someone who would stop at nothing to get what he wanted.

This caricature of John Paul Jones as a pirate was made around 1779. It demonstrates the worst of the fears of the British during his raids along the English coast.

7 The *Bonhomme Richard*

1779

Jones given
command of the
Bonhomme Richard

Not long after he had taken the *Drake,* Jones steered the *Ranger* back to France. One of his first missions was to get money to pay his crew, or at least to get food and clothing for them. During his time in the Continental navy, Jones tried several times to get money to pay his men and supplies to keep them happy. But Congress was more concerned with supplying the Continental army than the Continental navy. The army was suffering greatly, especially in 1778, after the long, harsh winter at Valley Forge, Pennsylvania, during which 2,000 soldiers died of disease. Soldiers were cold, sick, and hungry, and Congress had to find money to buy food, blankets, uniforms, and other supplies for them. The navy, Congress decided, would have to wait.

Besides begging Congress for money, Jones also talked with Antoine de Sartine, the man in the French government who was in charge of **maritime** affairs. Jones told him about all the things he could do against the British if he had a better ship. The French considered the British among their greatest enemies, and they were eager to take away some of their power by weakening them. So Sartine told Jones that he would find him a larger, faster ship to use in his raids.

When he finally got the ship, however, Jones was disappointed. Instead of the shiny new ship he envisioned, Jones was presented with an old ship called the *Duc de Duras.* The ship had been used to sail to and from China for fourteen years, and it still smelled of the spices it had carried. While Jones had hoped to get a mighty warship, the *Duc de Duras* was a **merchant** trader with no guns. Still,

Jones knew he could change the ship so that it would come close to what he had hoped for.

One of the first things Jones did was to change the name of the ship to the *Bonhomme Richard.* In French, Bonhomme means "good man" or "good-natured fellow," and "Richard" was in honor of Benjamin Franklin, who Jones greatly admired as a friend and adviser. The name came from a character Franklin had created in 1732 and featured in his popular publication, called *Poor Richard's Almanac.* Poor Richard—actually Ben Franklin, writing as Poor Richard—was a simple country man who came up with sayings such as "Early to bed and early to rise, makes a man healthy, wealthy, and wise." Many of his sayings are still used today.

The fleet leaves France

To prepare his new ship for battle, Jones mounted 40 guns on its decks. He painted the ship black and had new quarters put in for his officers. The

The *Bonhomme Richard* is seen here as painted in 1779. The crew included 150 American seaman. One hundred of them had recently been exchanged as prisoners of war for captured English sailors.

Jones and his ships set sail from the Isle de Groix, off the coast of France, on August 14, 1779. That same day they captured two trading ships in the English Channel.

French added to Jones's fleet by giving him four smaller ships as well. They were the *Alliance, Pallas, Vengeance,* and *Cerf.*

On August 14, 1779, the fleet left France for Great Britain. Jones was in command of all the ships, but he remained on the *Bonhomme Richard.* Each of the other ships had her own captain, and each captain was supposed to take orders from Jones. The orders were usually given by using signal flags. Sometimes, if a ship came close enough to the *Bonhomme Richard,* Jones could use a speaking tube to shout orders across the waves.

Not long after the fleet set sail, Jones and Captain Landais, who was the captain of the *Alliance,* had a disagreement. Jones told Landais he could not go after a prize he wanted to pursue.

Ships Jones commanded

Ship name	Year took command
John	1767
Betsy	1772
Alfred	1775
Providence	1776
Ranger	1777
Bonhomme Richard	1779
Ariel	1780

Jones realized that the ship Landais wanted to capture was trying to damage the *Alliance* by leading her into the rocks. Later, Jones tried to smooth things over, but Captain Landais grew even angrier after Jones quietly accused him of lying. He challenged Jones to a **duel,** but Jones refused to fight him. After that, Captain Landais refused to pay attention to anything Jones ordered him to do. Later, this would create quite a problem, especially on September 23, 1779, when Jones engaged in the greatest sea battle of his career.

The ship *Alliance* was actually built in Salisbury, Massachusetts, and first sailed in 1778. The *Alliance* had 32 guns.

8 The Fight with *Serapis*

1779

September 23
Jones has a fierce
battle with the
British ship
Serapis, and is
victorious

John Paul Jones loved the sea and being a sailor. But he also loved the idea of being a hero; someone who earned a lot of honor and glory. Jones was always on the lookout for opportunities to do something that would gain him the attention he craved. It was not until September 23, 1779, however, that he finally got his chance to be a hero.

The *Bonhomme Richard* was cruising along the eastern coast of England that day, looking for prizes. It had been spotted by lookouts on shore who put out a red warning flag on Scarborough Castle. British Captain Richard Pearson spotted the warning as he was leading a **convoy** of 44 merchant ships on their way from Scandinavia to southern England. The ships carried naval supplies for England's Royal Navy. The lead ship in the convoy was Pearson's warship, the *Serapis.*

A few hours after seeing the warning flag, Captain Pearson spotted the four ships in Jones's **squadron.** He decided to protect the merchant ships by placing the *Serapis* and the other warship that was traveling with him, the *Countess of Scarborough*, between the American ships and the convoy.

Jones quickly realized that the convoy was carrying naval supplies, and that if he could capture even just some of the ships, he would become famous. He ordered his ships to raise all their sails they could catch as much wind as possible. Then the *Bonhomme Richard* and the other ships in the squadron began to prepare for battle.

Preparing for battle

To prepare, the sailors removed anything that could be moved from the decks, including chairs, tables, and bunks, and put them in the ships' holds. Then they sprinkled the decks with sand to absorb the blood they knew would be shed. While they were working up on deck, other men were busy below, putting out tubs for the **surgeons** on board to use. Naval warfare was a grim and violent experience, and all the men knew that at least a few of them would lose an arm or a leg before the day ended. The surgeons would **amputate** limbs that were destroyed beyond repair. The limbs would be put into the tubs, then taken up on deck and tossed overboard.

The battle begins

At about five o'clock, drummers began beating their drums as a call to battle. Jones knew the battle would be a hard one, but he expected to win. He had four ships to Pearson's two, and combined he had 120 guns. At six o'clock, an officer raised three flags to signal to his other ships to "form line of battle." But then Captain Landais, who had been giving Jones trouble for weeks, turned his ship,

This painting shows the *Bonhomme Richard* and the *Serapis* drawing closer together before the fighting began.

the *Alliance*, away. Another ship in Jones's squadron, the *Pallas*, ignored Jones's orders and continued sailing in a straight line. The fourth ship, *Vengeance,* stayed back. (Later, the *Pallas* returned to fight the *Countess of Scarborough*.) Jones became angry at the actions of his officers, but he did not change his mind about winning the battle. Now it was up to one ship to earn the victory—the *Bonhomme Richard*.

It was beginning to get dark as the sailors prepared for battle. Besides the guns mounted on the ships, they also had pistols and other weapons they could hold in their hands. The plan was for some sailors to climb the masts and shoot from on high, aiming at the enemy below them. Because the other three ships in Jones's **squadron** had **deserted** him, the number of guns on deck had gone down from 120 to the 40 guns on the *Bonhomme Richard*.

Captain Pearson drew the *Serapis* close enough to the *Bonhomme Richard* so that he could shout across to Jones. He asked Jones where his ship was from, but Jones did not answer. Then Pearson shouted, "Tell me instantly from whence you came and who you be, or I'll fire a broadside into you!"

The *Bonhomme Richard* and *Serapis* were lashed together and engaged in fierce, close-up fighting when the *Alliance* showed up and fired its guns, damaging both ships. The *Bonhomme Richard* began to sink, and Jones's situation became more desperate.

Jones had been flying British flags to trick the enemy into coming close and asking just such a question. When Pearson called out to him, Jones ordered the British flag lowered and the Continental navy flag raised. Now Pearson knew that he was facing a ship from the American navy, and because of John Paul Jones's reputation, he probably knew who was in charge of the ship. Suddenly one of the men aboard the *Bonhomme Richard* shot his gun, and all of the guns seemed to respond at once. Because the ships were so close, few of the shots missed. At one point, one of the guns on the *Bonhomme Richard* exploded, killing several men and burning others.

For more than two hours the two ships fought. A large crowd had gathered on shore and watched as the ships did a kind of dance in the water, brushing and ramming into each other. Because it was a newer and better-built ship, the *Serapis* could sail more quickly. As time passed, the *Bonhomme Richard* became heavily damaged, and Jones knew that he had to act quickly if he hoped to capture the enemy warship. The ships were right next to each other, and Jones noticed that one of the strong ropes from a mast on the *Serapis* was hanging across one of the decks of the *Bonhomme Richard*. He climbed up a mast, grabbed the rope, and tied it to one of the masts on the *Bonhomme Richard*. Then he ordered one of his officers to help him lash the two ships together even more securely. Next, the men on the *Bonhomme Richard* used **grappling hooks** to tangle up more ropes from the *Serapis*. The *Bonhomme Richard* was damaged so badly that Jones knew it could not be saved. If the ship started to sink, Captain Pearson would take Jones and his men aboard the *Serapis* and make them prisoners of war. Jones was determined not to let this happen. But he did not want to damage the *Serapis* more than he already had because he still intended to take it as a prize and make its crew his prisoners.

Suddenly, another ship came into view and began to shoot at the lashed-together ships. It was the *Alliance*, which under Captain Landais's command had deserted. Those on the *Bonhomme Richard* shouted for him to stop, but the guns kept firing. Later, Landais claimed that he had shot only at *Serapis*. But his shots had added to the damage already done to the *Bonhomme Richard*, and it started to sink. Frightened, an officer named Henry Gardner looked around to see what would happen next. He could see no other officers, and figured the others were all dead. So he shouted loudly the word for surrender—"Quarters!" But when Captain Pearson asked if the *Bonhomme Richard* was surrendering, John Paul Jones suddenly appeared to answer him.

Jones will not surrender

Legend says that Jones responded by shouting, "I have not yet begun to fight!" But no one is sure that he said such a thing. Still, what he did say was close enough—Jones refused to surrender. The fighting continued and grew even more violent as each side grew desperate. British sailors jumped aboard the *Bonhomme Richard* and used swords and pistols to fight the Americans. But when they realized that many Americans were still alive and angry enough to fight back fiercely, they went back to the *Serapis*. American sailors stationed on a small platform high above the deck shot and killed many of them with their pistols. Then a sailor from the *Bonhomme Richard* tossed a bomb into a hatch of the *Serapis*, setting off **ammunition** that was stored there. The *Serapis* caught on fire, and Captain Pearson finally surrendered. It was 10:30 P.M. and Jones had his prize. His ship was sinking, so he and his men boarded the *Serapis*, taking more than 100 English sailors prisoner. Added to the number he had taken on previous

John Paul Jones's supposed reply to Pearson, "I have not yet begun to fight," became the stuff of legend and has become a famous slogan of the U.S. navy. The event was dramatically recreated in this painting.

This is a picture of 18th-century Amsterdam, much as it would have looked when John Paul Jones arrived with his prize, the British warship *Serapis*.

raids—they had been kept in the hold of the *Bonhomme Richard* and were now transferred to the *Serapis*—he had about 500 prisoners in all.

While historians are not exactly sure how many men were killed, they have figured that about half the men on each ship died in the battle. Each ship had about 300 men on board, so all together about 300 were killed.

Three days later, Jones, his crew, and his prisoners had all transferred to the *Serapis* and were ready to sail back to France or to the closest **neutral** territory, the Dutch coast. But guard ships were sailing up and down the coast of England, planning to stop him. For ten days the *Serapis* sailed to and fro to avoid being caught. Somehow Jones managed to sail the ship safely to Holland with his prize. In the Dutch city of Amsterdam, Jones was greeted just as he had hoped—as a hero. He was cheered and surrounded by crowds who asked him questions about the battle. People ran up to him on the streets and hugged and kissed him. He had conquered a British warship, something few sea captains could claim.

Sixty-nine years too late

In 1848 Congress finally voted to award the crew of the *Bonhomme Richard* prize money for the ships they captured. By that time, all of the men who had sailed on the *Bonhomme Richard* were dead. The money totaled $165,598.37 and was given to the **descendants** of the crew members.

9 A Fading Career

With his victory over *Serapis*, Captain John Paul Jones had gained the glory and honor that he had desired for so long. The battle of September 23, 1779, was the one that made Jones a legend. In Great Britain he was both feared and admired. In America he was a hero.

Jones wrote an account of the battle for his friend Benjamin Franklin, who sent copies of the account to newspapers in both the United States and Europe. When the story was published, Jones became even more famous.

Jones remained in Amsterdam for more than two months. One thing he had hoped to do while there was to work out a prisoner exchange wherein American prisoners would be set free in exchange for the British prisoners he had captured. He was not able to work out an exchange, but he enjoyed his stay in Amsterdam. Because he was considered a hero, Jones was a guest at many parties.

Meanwhile, the American sailors who had fought with Jones were unhappy. They felt that he was ignoring them while enjoying the city of Amsterdam. Many of them had suffered wounds in the battle, some very severe, and they remained aboard the *Serapis*, the well tending the wounded. Also, they wondered when—if ever—they would be paid for the work they had done for the Continental navy. Some members of Jones's **squadron** also disliked him because they felt he took most of the glory for himself and gave little credit to those who had fought just as hard—or harder— than he had in the battle.

In December 1779, Jones sailed back to France. He went to Paris to try to get payment and prize money for himself and

King Louis XVI of France, pictured here in 1775, gave his support to the cause of the United States. The French support was crucial for the success of the American fight for independence from Great Britain.

his men, but he was not successful. While in France, he visited many government officials and made sure they knew the details of the fight between the *Bonhomme Richard* and *Serapis*. Before he left Paris, the French government awarded Jones the Order of Military Merit, and French King Louis XVI presented him with a gold sword. Jones highly prized the sword and kept it at his side for most of his life. Today the sword is displayed next to Jones's tomb in Annapolis, Maryland.

While in France, Jones received orders from Benjamin Franklin to take a shipload of supplies for the Continental army back to the United States, but

Challenged to a duel

While in a **tavern** in Amsterdam, Jones and Landais ran into each other. They continued their quarrel, and Landais again challenged Jones to a **duel.** Jones replied that he would rather have their issues settled in court and walked away. Landais later captained the supply ship *Alliance,* which Jones was originally supposed to sail back to America. On the voyage, Landais had a nervous breakdown and had to be carried off the ship. He was later dismissed from the navy.

he did not even want to see his crew again until he had money for them. He hesitated for so long that American leaders began to get very frustrated with him, because he did not seem to want to sail the supply ship back to the United States. Jones finally sailed the ship *Ariel* back to Philadelphia in December 1780.

Back in America

Back in the United States, Congress told Jones it had decided to make him captain of a new ship, called *America*. The ship was being built in Portsmouth, New Hampshire, and Jones went to see it. *America* was a fine ship, and Jones was excited to sail it. In fact, he was so worried that British soldiers would try to burn it that he personally guarded it at night. And when Congress ran out of money to finish building *America*, Jones paid the workmen himself. But he was soon disappointed, because Congress decided that instead of keeping the ship and making Jones its captain, they would give it to France to thank that country for helping them in the Revolutionary War. Then the war officially ended in 1783, marking the end of Jones's career in the American navy.

After the war, Congress decided to pay Jones back wages totaling about $21,000. Then Jones became very sick, and he went to the mountains of Pennsylvania to recover. As his health improved, he came up with many ideas for how to build up the American navy and make it one of the best in the world. He offered his services to Congress, telling them he would be happy to work for the navy in any way he could. But Congress at that time was not that interested in the navy. They were still trying to pay for the war.

In 1784, Jones returned again to Paris to try to get money for the men who had fought on the *Bonhomme Richard* and the *Ranger*. Before he arrived in Paris, however, he stopped off in England. He had been given secret letters to give to **Ambassador** John Adams, who was in London. Jones was taking a great risk, because he was a wanted man in England. If he had been recognized and captured, he would have been put on trial and quite possibly severely punished—even hanged—for his actions against the British.

Also in 1784, Jones brought with him the sack of silver that his men had stolen from the home of the Earl of Selkirk in 1778. He returned the silver to the Earl with a long letter in which he apologized for the theft. He also sent messages to British newspapers telling them that he had returned the silver, and they printed articles about it.

In the summer of 1785, Jones went back to America. Congress rewarded him for his bravery by giving him a gold medal. But his fame was fading. He looked around for something to do, something that would make him famous again. He got an idea of what to do next from Thomas Jefferson, the American ambassador in Paris and future U.S. president. Soon, Jones was on his way to Russia.

This is the medal Congress awarded to John Paul Jones for his service during the Revolutionary War. One side features a portrait of Jones (left) with a Latin inscription that translates as "The American Congress to John Paul Jones, Commander of the Fleet."

The other side of the medal (right) shows the *Bonhomme Richard* on fire, with the crew boarding the damaged *Serapis*. The inscription translates as "The enemy's ships captured or put to flight at Scotland's shore September 23, 1779."

10 Last Years and Legacy

In November 1787, Jones returned to Paris, where he met with Thomas Jefferson. Jefferson knew that Jones wanted to be back at sea and told him that the **empress** of Russia, Catherine the Great, wanted to hire naval commanders. She wanted them to help her to take the land of Constantinople from the Turks, who had ruled it for 300 years, and give it to her son to rule.

At first John Paul Jones did not think he should go to Russia. But the Russian **ambassador** helped him change his mind. Jones joined the Russian navy in 1788, when he was 40 years old. He was successful in battle, but the Russian court was full of deception, and people spread rumors about one another in order to gain the favor of the empress. In 1789 Jones was forced to leave Russia after being accused of a crime. Most historians agree that he did not commit the crime, but Jones could not prove otherwise.

John Paul Jones spent his last years in Paris. His health was poor during those years—he often suffered from **pneumonia,** probably from spending so much time on the open sea in damp conditions. He tried to recapture his former glory, but could not. On July 18, 1792, Jones died. The French government buried him in a Paris cemetery, but in 1796 the cemetery was sold and forgotten. In 1899, the American ambassador to France decided to find where Jones was buried. In 1905 his grave was finally discovered, and U.S. President Theodore Roosevelt had his body brought

Catherine the Great of Russia was anxious to expand her empire and fought the Ottoman Turks to do so. John Paul Jones briefly served as rear admiral in the Black Sea fleet, fighting for Catherine against the Turks.

The body of John Paul Jones rests in a marble sarcophagus under the Naval Academy Chapel in Annapolis, Maryland.

back to the United States. A tomb was built inside the Naval Academy Chapel in Annapolis, Maryland, and Jones's body was placed inside during a ceremony.

Legacy

Jones was a role model for naval officers during his lifetime and even up to modern times. Because he was sometimes seen as cold and too demanding, he was not always a good leader. But while his character was not always admired, he was brave in the face of battle and willing to fight to the end.

Perhaps Jones's greatest legacy was his faith in the U.S. navy. He believed that the navy could equal or even be better than any other in the world. Jones wrote many documents outlining his ideas for improving the standards and training of the navy, and most of his ideas were good ones.

Today, Jones might well be surprised at how powerful the navy he loved has become. Almost 400,000 people are now in the United States navy. The navy has more than 300 ships and submarines. And most of the ships are hundreds of times larger and faster than the *Ranger*, the *Providence*, or the *Bonhomme Richard*.

President Roosevelt praises John Paul Jones

When the body of John Paul Jones was brought to the Chapel at the U.S. Naval Academy on April 24, 1906, then-President Theodore Roosevelt made a speech in which he said:

> The future naval officers, who live within these walls, will find in the career of the man whose life we this day celebrate, not merely a subject for admiration and respect, but an object lesson to be taken into their innermost hearts. . . . Every officer . . . should feel in each fiber of his being an eager desire to emulate the energy, the professional capacity, the indomitable determination and dauntless scorn of death which marked John Paul Jones above all his fellows.

Timeline

July 6, 1747	John Paul born in Kirkcudbrightshire, Scotland
1760	Paul became an **apprentice** on the ship *Friendship*
1764	Paul became a member of the crew on the slave ship *King George*
1766	Paul became a crew member on the slave ship *Two Friends*
1768	Paul made captain of the *John;* arrested for murder of Mungo Maxwell
1773	Paul became captain of the *Betsy;* he fought with the Ringleader, during which the Ringleader was killed; Paul escaped to Virginia and added "Jones" to his name
April 1775	Battles at Lexington and Concord, which mark the start of the Revolutionary War; Jones joined the Continental navy; given command of the *Alfred*
December 1775	Jones became the first to hoist the Grand Union flag on an American naval ship
May 10, 1776	Jones appointed to command the *Providence*
July 2, 1776	Congress voted to declare independence from Great Britain
July 4, 1776	Congress announced the Declaration of Independence
November 1777	Jones sailed to France in the *Ranger;* met with Benjamin Franklin
February 6, 1778	French decided to help the United States win the war
February 14, 1778	Jones was saluted by French Admiral La Motte-Picquet
April 24, 1778	Jones captured the British warship *Drake*
1779	France loaned the *Bonhomme Richard* to Jones
September 23, 1779	Jones engaged in a fight with the *Serapis* and was victorious
September 25, 1779	The *Bonhomme Richard* sank
December 1779	Jones sailed to France, where he was treated as a hero and was accepted into French society
1780	Jones given command of the *Ariel*; sailed to Philadelphia
1781	Jones told he would command the *America* after it was built; later, the *America* was instead given to France
October 19, 1781	British General Cornwallis surrendered to General George Washington at Yorktown, Virginia
December 1782	Jones returned to France to join in a planned invasion of Jamaica, but it was called off
February 4, 1783	England announced that the Revolutionary War was officially over
May 1783	Jones returned to Philadelphia

November 1783	Jones returned to France to try to get prize money for himself and his crew
1787	Jones returned to United States
March 1788	Jones joined the Russian navy
April 1788	Jones arrived in Russia
1790	Jones returned to Paris; George Washington offered him a military position, but Jones was too ill to accept it
July 18, 1792	John Paul Jones died

Further Reading

Hossell, Karen Price. *The Boston Tea Party: Rebellion in the Colonies.* Chicago: Heinemann Library, 2003.

Hossell, Karen Price. *The Declaration of Independence.* Chicago: Heinemann Library, 2004.

Lutz, Norma Jean. *John Paul Jones: Father of the U.S. Navy.* Broomall, Penn.: Chelsea House Publishing, 2000.

Smolinski, Diane. *Important People of the Revolutionary War.* Chicago: Heinemann Library, 2002.

Smolinski, Diane. *Naval Warfare of the Revolutionary War.* Chicago: Heinemann Library, 2002.

Tibbits, Alison Davis. *John Paul Jones: Father of the American Navy.* Berkeley Heights, N.J.: Enslow Publishers, Inc., 2002.

Glossary

ale alcoholic drink similar to beer

alliance friendly agreement to work together

ambassador person from one country sent on a government mission to another country

ammunition bullets, cartridges, and other items to be shot from guns

amputate cut off

apprentice someone who promises to work for a set amount of time for someone else while learning a skill or trade

bayonet steel blade that attaches to the end of a rifle or musket (gun used in Revolutionary War that is similar to a rifle)

capsize turn over

colonist person who lives in a colony

colony settlement in a new territory that is tied to an established nation

commissioner representative of a government sent to take care of matters in another country

commodore captain in navy in command of a squadron

compromise work out an agreement wherein all parties are satisfied but none gets exactly what he or she wants

Continental Congress group of representatives from the colonies who carried out the duties of the government

convoy group of ships or trucks traveling together

cruiser large, fast warship with guns

descendant someone who belongs to a later generation of the same family

desert, deserter someone who escapes military duty without permission

duel battle fought with weapons between two persons; duels have formal rules and require witnesses

empress woman who is in charge of an empire

escort go along with something to ensure its safety

first lieutenant in the navy, the officer responsible for making sure the ship is in good condition

grappling hook hook with long handle used to pull ships to each other or to pull objects out of the water

guild association of merchants or craftspeople with common interests who come together for mutual support and aid

jury group of people selected to attend a trial and determine, based on what they hear, whether a person is guilty of a crime

loyalist someone who remains loyal to a particular cause; during the American Revolution, a Loyalist was someone who remained loyal to Great Britain

maritime having to do with the sea

merchant shop owner or trader

merchantmen ships carrying goods to be sold by merchants

militia citizens banded together in a military unit

mutiny refusal to obey authority, especially in a military situation

negotiation process of discussion and compromise with another party to achieve a goal

neutral not taking sides in a conflict

Parliament supreme lawmaking body in Great Britain

Patriot person who supports his or her country; during the American Revolution, those who fought for freedom from Great Britain

piracy actions of pirates

plantation large farm on which crops are tended by laborers who also live there

privateer ship licensed to attack private shipping, or someone who works on a privateer ship

promotion being put in a higher position or made more important

prospect possibility; something that could occur in the future

ransom something paid to ensure the return of something or someone held captive

recruit find new members; one of those new members is called a recruit

seizure sudden attack and capture

sloop boat with one mast and one sail

smallpox disease that causes fever and markings on the skin; in past times, many people died of smallpox

stonemason person who builds things with stone

squadron naval unit of two or more divisions

surgeon doctor who performs operations

tavern building in which alcoholic beverages are sold; in colonial times, taverns were more like inns, where alcoholic beverages and food were sold and rooms were rented out

third mate deck officer on a merchant ship

Tobago island in the Caribbean, off the coast of South America

tyranny harsh government in which one ruler has all the power

Index